YES DAY!

Amy Krouse Rosenthal & Tom Lichtenheld

HarperCollinsPublishers

Just watch, you'll see what I mean. . . .

Can I please have
pizza for breakfast?

Can I use
your hair gel?

Can I clean my room tomorrow?

Can I pick?

Can we get ice cream?

Can I eat lunch outside?

Can we have a food fight?

Can we invent our own game?

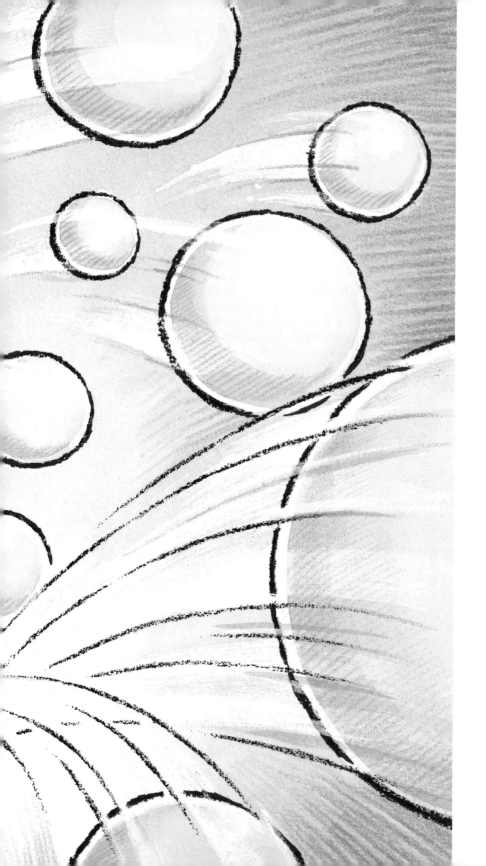

Can I have a
piggyback ride?

Can Mario come
over for dinner?

Can we stay up *really* late?

Does this day have to end?

The End
(of Yes Day)

See you again
next year!